MEDITATE TO
UNLOCK AWARENESS

MEDITATE TO UNLOCK AWARENESS

EDNA E. CRAVEN, DC, CTN, BCI, ME

This Book Is Dedicated

In Loving Memory of

Thomas Arthur Lisemby, III
1938-2017

Since the moment I saw You, I loved You
My beloved Friend, My Lover, My Confidant
You helped me understand God, His ways
I glanced at the Spirit and saw your glorious Soul

CONTENTS

FOREWORD

Ceremony and rituals have long played a vital and essential role in our culture. We consider spirituality an integral part of our very being. We embrace ceremonies and rituals that gives us the power to conquer the difficulties of life, as well as in events and in milestones, such as puberty, marriage, and death.

We witness how the church uses rituals or performs solemn ceremonies consisting of a series of actions according to a prescribed order. Similarly, a series of actions or type of behavior regularly and invariably are followed by people when praying, in inauguration ceremonies, in ribbon cuttings, in taking oaths, in standing when a Judge enters the court room, in pledging allegiance to the flag of a nation, in standing and singing the national anthem, or when observing a moment of silence to honor fallen heroes, and when burying the dead. These are just a few examples of people performing rituals. Ritual has, is, and will always be in and around us.

The need for ritual is more apparent in prayer. Some people kneel, clasp their hands, bow, and utter silently words of prayer. Others raise their arms toward the heavens while praying to God. Others kiss the floor in sign of humility. Still, others wash their hands and feet, burn incense, light a candle, and solemnly enter into meditation.

Since childhood I was exposed to meditation rituals. I observed my mother, how she incensed the whole house and lighted candles before she retired into a closet to meditate and later emerged from that closet looking refreshed, rejuvenated. Often, I listened to vowel sounds she played before she went into meditation.

She also let my brother and I light candles before she read us mystical stories. My brother and I took turns in snuffing out the candles, which I enjoyed. Every night she led us into praying *The Great Invocation* and spent time explaining its meaning. These were extraordinary moments that helped mold my spiritual being. I am grateful she afforded me such uplifting opportunities early in life. They have deepened my sense of Self and have opened my intelligence to receive experiential knowledge of God.

It gives me great pleasure to see that my mother has written this book, *Meditate To Unlock Awareness*, for she knows this subject very well. She has been practicing meditation since 1968 and has been involved in mysticism and arcane science for more than 5 decades. She voluntarily entered the spiritual path while she was still a teenager. Her vast knowledge on meditation

practices has culminated in the writing of this book, *Meditate To Unlock Awareness*, a methodology to a successful meditation practice.

I am a family man, with a beautiful wife and 3 lovely children. Professionally, I am a seasoned entrepreneur with extensive experience in organization and business development. My entrepreneurial skills encompass the Cheerleading Industry, both, as a competitor, and as a coach. I attained the NCA 2002 Collegiate National Title—with the rest of my cheerleader team members. I received a cheerleading safety certification from the AACCA Safety Association, which is a nationally recognized authoritative source on cheerleading safety. I acquired three other safety certifications: one from the United States Association of Gymnastics (Level 1-5); the other two are in CPR and First Aid. In 2004, I opened up my own gymnastics and cheerleading athletic center. Subsequently, I sold the business as a going concern after 14 years of dedication.

My entrepreneurial abilities also extend to housing restoration, investments, and financial management. In addition, I aspire to pursue a law degree following a strong desire to serve my community in this capacity.

I graduated with honors and distinctions from Tarrant County College (TCC) and received an Associate degree in Arts and Certification in Network Administration. I acquired another degree in International Studies with emphasis on business from Southern Methodist University (SMU). During my studentship, I was a member of the Phi Theta Kappa National Honor Society, became a Student Ambassador, and received the Exceptional Leadership Award, the Spirit of Southeast Award, and the TCC Service Award. I was nominated and became the President of the executive board of TAMACS and held the Fundraising Chair. Further, I was the Events' Coordinator for Omega Delta Phi International Fraternity, Inc. and was the Chair Person for the 2001 SMU Political Issues Forum.

As you can see, I have kept myself busy and till this day continue in this mode of being for I enjoy doing a lot of different things. Sometimes my schedule gets very full and it is easy to get caught up in "doing" without taking notice of what is being sacrificed, even though "doing" may actually be in my best interest. When so, I do minor adjustments to help me enjoy the ride more. But, sometimes I need to make major changes to ensure I don't compromise my happiness, which on occasions I have. A key factor for me has been to take time to be with myself to maintain my center, my sense of joy, and align my goals with my values. Meditation affords me this opportunity. It brings me into accord, harmony, or sympathetic relationship with living.

Meditation has taught me how to decompress, how to shut off my worldly mind, how to expel less mental energy, and how to give myself a break from the constant hustles I face in working life. I find meditation to be a good practice in my life, a practice I need to constantly work at. It is especially helpful when I am overwhelmingly busy. *Meditate To Unlock Awareness* equips me with tools to handle the challenges I face and to call the shots in my life.

The Great Invocation

From the point of Light within the Mind of God,
Let Light stream forth into the minds of men.
Let Light descend on Earth.
From the point of Love within the Heart of God,
Let Love stream forth into the hearts of men.
May Christ return to Earth.
From the centre where the Will of God is known,
Let purpose guide the Little Wills of men,
The purpose which the Masters know and serve.
From the centre, which we call the race of men,
Let the plan of Love and Light work out,
And may it seal the door where evil dwells.
Let Light and Love and Power restore the Plan on Earth.

Nicholas Glenn Craven
Weatherford, Texas

PREFACE

Among all of the social and business engagements that we busy ourselves, making a determination and effort to know the right law for which our being is governed is the most important.

Like children, we can always experience joy and peace, but it is very difficult for our mind to reclaim that joy and peace after it has fallen into the hands of restlessness and material desires. This book, *Meditate To Unlock Awareness*, has been created to help you make spiritual hay while your readiness to meditate excels; to help you make the best use of time and opportunity by overcoming existing states of limitations and by expanding your consciousness through the use of specific techniques of meditation that can help you develop the power to control your destiny, and prevent failure and disease.

Increasing our inner stability and strength rest in observing and comprehending our creative, involutionary and evolutionary processes. *Meditate To Unlock Awareness* portrays three forms of of turning inwards to allow for serious contemplation of your creative forces, of your emotions, mental operations, and desires, to produce results that go beyond the lower mind—which is the biggest obstacle standing between your awareness and yourself—and experience your true nature, described as peace, happiness, and bliss.

My experiences and realizations gained from over 50 years of meditation and studying arcane sciences, which began with the Ancient Mystical Order Rosae Crucis, has culminated in the writing of this book, to help the reader Meditate To Unlock Awareness so that all queries be resolved and the darkness of ignorance may forever be dispelled by the light that shines within and that can be accessed through meditation.

ACKNOWLEDGMENT

My deepest gratitude goes to:

- GOD for having used me as an instrument to make this book possible.
- My son, Nicholas G. Craven, for his thoughtful and loving contribution to the Foreword, for his encouragement to write this book, and for voicing contributing ideas.
- My cosmic friend and benefactor Robert K. Krauth for his value assistance in editing my work, for his contributing ideas in the writing of this book, and for his financial support. Robert's friendship is one of a kind consisting in being useful. He rejoices in the good fortune of our friendship and gladly foregoes self-interest for the sake of our sacred work, without consciousness of loss or sacrifice.
- My dearest friend, Lillie White, for being instrumental in editing my work and voicing constructive criticism. Our deep friendship goes back over 40 years and during this time, she has been a great influence in things of the Spirit and very inspiring.

INTRODUCTION

Don't say that you are too busy with concerns, and the care of keeping the wolf from the door, to find time for the culture of stellar qualities. Helping expand and deepening our consciousness is everyone's responsibility. Our commitment with business is important, but our appointment to serve others is more important; and our commitment with our Creator, meditation, truth, and home is most important.

Joy is the aim of life. Material things do not bring us real joy, but temporary physical pleasures. Discontent usually follows. We find that indulging too much in earthly pleasure brings us unhappiness. It is like saying: "too much of a good thing is a bad thing." We reap the harvest of what we sow and we reward or punish ourselves according to the Law of Cause and Effect.[1] We find that only by living in harmony with Nature's laws do we accomplish the noble purpose of human living. Every good action that we performed—whether eating wholesome foods, resting, or living a clean life—digs deep into our consciousness and brings forth a small amount of joy. However, to merely live and then die at the end of our living seems futile, unless we have taken good action to expand our consciousness, to bring forth greater joy in our lives. Meditation, which is the highest form of good action, opens the door of consciousness and lets the joy of life pour out. We discover that in meditation, bliss continuously comes forth and bathes our soul, the spiritual center of our Higher Self.

---

[1]   Cause and Effect is the Law of Retribution: repayment or return accommodated to our actions.

1

THE ART OF MEDITATION

"You are the only person you can ever know intimately. You are the one with whom you must live eternally. The greatest gift Life could have made to you is yourself. You are a spontaneous, self-choosing center in Life, in the great drama of being, the great joy of becoming, the certainty of eternal expansion. You could not ask for more and more could not have been given."

Ernest Holmes

When you think of spiritually expanding yourself, you are setting intentions to up your level of understanding and make definite shifts in your life. New inspirational ideas come to you, you feel fearless, powerful and strong, intuitive. These feelings usually begin to occur when you are in the relaxed state of meditation and willing to search actively for evidence against your favored beliefs, and to weigh such evidence fairly when it is available.

It is proven that meditation can help eliminate negative thoughts, worries, anxiety, and all factors that can prevent you from feeling happy. So, what is medication?

"Meditation is the art of close and continued thought; it is a turning or revolving of a subject in the mind"[1]. It is a form of concentration to consciously tune in with Cosmic Consciousness to reinforce, revitalize, and strengthen your human faculties with celestial ones, through faithful, persevering practice. With the exception of some extra-sensory perceptions and paranormal events or phenomena such as clairvoyance, which are beyond the scope of normal scientific understanding, in meditation, the revolving subject is always under your control, your mental operations. Your thinking influences it and it is treated and handled based on your conceptions.

---

[1]   Webster, LLD, Noah. New Twentieth Century Dictionary (unabridged), 1946

We meditate for various reasons. One principal reason is to know God more intimately, to commune with Him. Another is to lift us above material circumstances, above routine and all littleness, and still another, is to help us know our true selves, who we truly are spiritually.

There exist various forms of turning inward to allow for serious contemplation of your emotions, your mental operations, and your desires. Three simple steps can be exercised to lead you to the ever-new joy of meditation.

1. By observation
2. By methodical experimentation, and
3. By self-analysis

By observation

When diving deep into the mute cravings of your inner self, you can observe the perpetual current of thoughts and emotions that arise within you. Are they benign? Are they revitalizing? Are they discerning? Are they visionary? Do they enlarge your consciousness? Take mental notes of your observations. You may for example, pay attention to an occurrence (situation or event) presented for observation in your mind with its attendant circumstances and conditions. Then, follow what you observed by recording such scrutiny. Logging the experience can shed light when you revisit the observation in writing allowing you to seize the higher meaning or valuable lesson inherent in the occurrence.

By methodical experimentation

Through experimentation, you can try to discover some unknown truth, principle, or effect about yourself and establish it when you discover it. For example, you can try to find the good (pearls of wisdom, divine joy) and the beauty within you as you withdraw into your own soul (the holy place) as opposed to going outside into the manifold (usually by laborious productions) to attract things you think are beautiful in the material world. When you come to the realization that going into the manifold to find beauty does not bring real joy, you can then forsake it for your soul and so float upward toward the divine fount of being, whose stream floats within you.

You can also experiment using tools (refer to Chapter 7) to improve your life in different capacities, to create vibratory conditions conducive to the attainments of your goals, and to invoke potencies to awake higher powers within your mind and consciousness to lead you to a thorough knowledge of yourself.

By self-analysis

What do you know about yourself? Who are you really? Being aware of yourself is an important first step in knowing who you are as an individual. This entails noticing your thoughts, becoming aware of your perceptions, recognizing your feelings, analyzing your core values, your real motives for doing things, your character—your peculiarities, your nature, your distinctive qualities; what distinguish you from others. Then, you can work at getting rid of the nemesis of dark gloom you find within yourself. You can invoke a higher power, GOD, to teach you to behold only what is good, think only what is good, associate only with those who are good, and then, proceed to meditate upon Him, the fountain of all goodness.

Gradually, as you make sense of yourself (by meditation and prayer), you learn that your work is performed for you, in you, and through you, and that the fruitage is brought right to your doorstep. You cognize that your solemn request for assistance has been answered tangibly and visibly.

It is the writer's experience that with an ever-increasing joy of meditation prayers are answered. Further and as an added bonus, celestial perceptions can be picked up; that is, subtle sounds (cosmic music*) can be heard roaming in the universe as one tunes-in to these rates of vibration otherwise inaudible.

BEST MEDITATION PRACTICE

Chapter 6, 7, and 8 present to the reader revealing facts and ideas relevant to the three simple steps that can be taken into your meditation practice. Select carefully the method of meditation best adapted to your needs—whether by observation, by methodical experimentation or by self-analysis—and stick to it. Many people loose themselves in the different forms of meditations, moving from one type of meditation to another until they feel utterly bewildered. Determine now, from the very beginning, that you will give careful, practical attention to the processes and principles you have judiciously selected; and that with the help of this book, you will keep on learning and practicing until you are able to see the results in yourself.

---

*   Cosmic Music is also known as "Music of the Spheres"—a perfectly harmonious music thought by Pythagoras and later classical and medieval philosophers to be produced by the movement of celestial bodies but to be inaudible on the earth.

2

FINDING REPOSE

The average working person may use only about 25% of his or her powers of concentration to attain meditation. But, with continued practice he or she will be lead into the art of meditation and in addition learn to balance earthly success with spiritual success.

Aberrations must be done away with. In time, working people learn to calm their mind by preventing disturbing impressions from reaching their brain. They learn to disengage their attention from all impressions (i.e.: deadlines, business deals, etc.) and to focus it on any of the three modes of meditation—observation, methodical experimentation, or self-analysis—to achieve their spiritual goals.

Yet, we find that we do not have to be a working person to experience the dilemma of not being able to concentrate 100% on meditation. Many of us are seeking for ways to help us achieve a mentally clear and emotionally calm state. Our busy lives keep us in a state of flux making concentration a difficult task. So, what are our options? The answers lie in learning to calm our senses, to control our breath, and to calm our mind.

Calming Your Senses

Normally, the life force in the nervous system keeps you entrapped with impressions coming from the eyes, ears, hands, mouth, and nose, but quickly removing the life force from all consciousness of the body, frees your attention from the incoming impressions and concentration can successfully be reached. You do this by knowing what the impressions are, by switching your attention off from them, and by throwing your attention at will on what you wish to concentrate upon and holding it there uninterruptedly, for as long as you desire. Your breath plays a major role.

Watching Your Breath

All living creatures are ordained by Nature to breathe. If your body is starving for oxygen because of improper body posture, the need to breathe deeply is necessary. Sitting with a bent spine and walking with a caved-in chest squeezes the diaphragm and lungs and prevents them from properly expanding and receiving the amount of oxygen necessary to cleanse all the devitalized blood in the lungs and to maintain vitality in your body. Sit and walk with the chest out and the abdomen in, to take in the proper quantity of oxygen your body needs. Learn to breathe correctly by always keeping the spine straight.

In regular breathing you are seldom aware of whether you are inhaling or exhaling the breath. Watching the breath brings emotional stability amid trials and tribulations, and deep calmness and physical vigor to concentrate successfully on your spiritual work.

Begin by expelling your breath deliberately first, as a signal to mentally begin watching the breath or becoming aware of the incoming and outgoing breath without forcing it in or out. Do not try to control the flow of the breath in any way; merely oberve it. The purpose of this practice is to lengthen naturally the intervals when the breath does not flow. Wait and enjoy that state of breathlessness, which is calming, soothing. By watching the breath, you separate the ego from it and become a silent witness of bodily activities. You begin to understand that your body is only partially sustained by breath, that your body's battery is internally charged with Cosmic energy enabling the cells of your body to brim over with life force. You learn that in a state of breathlessness, the heart slows its action and calms down, which then switches off the energy in the five senses, the cause of much distraction.

Calming Your Mind

Calmed nerves, controlled bodily energy, and a regulated moral life usually attend mental calmness. You can quiet your body easily, but find that it is difficult to silence your thoughts. They still run wild, jumping from one thing to another with amazing speed. When the life force and the consciousness are withdrawn from the nerves that control the five senses, the sensations they create cannot reach the brain. When sensations stop entering the brain, their impressions and corresponding ideas cease. It is then that the mind becomes free to contemplate on any subject of your choice. By mentally watching the breath, you cause both your breath and your mind to become calm. Breathing is reduced to a minimum, and sensations from the five senses cease to trigger thoughts, which in turn cease to trigger the subconscious mind by correlated thoughts.

Your attention thus becomes free from all distractions, and you are ready to focus your mind on your meditation practice.

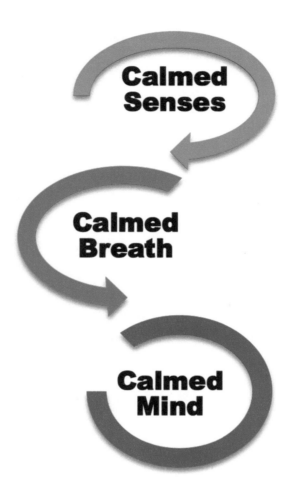

3

OVERCOMING NERVOUSNESS

Nervousness is an uncomfortable state of being that can get in the way of a successful meditation practice. If you are nervous, you cannot concentrate and work efficiently. You cannot meditate deeply to acquire peace and wisdom because nervousness interferes with all the normal functions of the human body and thinking ability, upsetting the physical, mental, and spiritual structures.

Many are the causes of nervousness. Restlessness in thinking sends surplus energy vibrating along the nerves. Excessive stimulation of the senses (as in drinking, overeating, unsound elimination, excitability, sexual permissiveness), prolonged fears, enmity, pessimism, bad conscience, sorrow, grudges, dissatisfaction, agitations, and lack of any of the necessities for normal and happy living (exercise, fresh air, sunshine, right food, enjoyable work, and a purpose in life) aggravate the condition. Fear, worry, and anger do the most damage to the nervous system. Worry and anger affect the whole body lessening brainpower and general efficiency of the nervous system. Prolonged fears affects the heart and may develop irregular heartbeats and other heart conditions. You voluntarily become victim of the fear and of the self-created destructive thought forms. Through self-suggestion within your own mind, you become not only enslaved by the fear but a ready victim of the unpleasantries your mind invents. Whatever fear you accept becomes law unto you. These fears translate themselves from a purely mental state into a dynamic physical power and force that carries on, unfolds, develops, and proceeds in accordance to your own thought processes and will only stop when you frustrate their activities by the same thought processes you used to bring them into existence. Calmly examine the cause to remove such disturbances and preserve yourself and your own wellbeing. Let God flow through you, and you will have all the power you need.

4

EMPOWERING YOUR SPIRITUAL POTENTIAL

Our actions bring about good when we guide our will with wisdom, not so, if we use our will ignorantly. Many people misconstrue the real meaning of "Thy will be done," and teach a troubling dogma of not using our will. Many others are physically lazy—and most people are mentally lazy. They are afraid even to initiate creative thinking, or self-emancipating thinking, lest they succeed.

Ordinarily, our will works within the boundaries of our own circle of family and friends, environment, world conditions, and cause-and-effect governed actions. This way of existing may go on for years, until through meditation we find the all-powerful divine will reigning within.

The Divine Mind assists us in discovering unknown truths, principles, or changes about ourselves and helps us establish them in our consciousness. The journey within makes us aware of some form of intelligence assisting us in this discovery, an indication we are participating in an active form of attunement with the Universal Mind of which you are a part.

As you enter into meditation, harness your will and activity to the right goal by contacting the Universal Mind first. But, you cannot make that contact if your mind is disordered by restlessness. You must repair your mind by practicing deep calmness. Then, give the Universal Mind a real soul-call, not giving up after only a few calls if you do not seem to make contact at first. You must continue transmitting your thoughts through your mental calmness until you sense the attunement.

Mental calmness

Exercising your body, strengthening your muscles (to include the heart), and purifying your bloodstream are important in your spiritual routine of meditation, for they will not only recharge your body with energy, but they will also help keep your body in a state of health and calmness that is conducive to meditation and the conscious control of your life force. Restlessness and sense perceptions will cease to be obstacles to the attainment of higher meditative states when you are well, have mastered mental calmness, and consciously control your life force, which enters your body with each breath you take.

Life force (also known as universal life force) interacts with your internal environment—stabilizing, balancing, and equilibrating your being to influence you positively or negatively depending if your breathing is out of control or balanced. If out of control, you experience excessive swings of energy that disturb and distort your psyche. If balanced, you facilitate easier, coordinated, integrated, and strengthened states of breathing and being (homeostasis) that propel and guide you toward the direction in meditation you care to go. In meditation, you find the breath and the life force automatically calmed, and thus long-term internal stability is attained. This denotes a state of poise or balance reached whereby you find repose.

5

PREPAREDNESS

Your Meditation Space

A small place used only for meditation is ideal and conducive to produce the inner silence you seek. Preferable, choose the same place every time you wish to meditate. Considering this place your temple, you will begin to permeate it with your vibrations as you use it repeatedly to meditate uninterruptedly. Charged with your vibrations, this place will promote a meditative state more rapidly.

In your meditation place put an armless straight chair of comfortable height facing in the direction best suited to induce the state of mind desired—East, West, North, South, Southeast, Southwest, Northeast, or Northwest. This will be your meditation seat (Figure 1).

Figure 1.

Cover your chair with a woolen blanket or a silk cloth so as to shield the back and the front of the seat and run down on the floor under your feet. Both, the wool and the silk covers will protect your body against underground currents, so that their opposing magnetic pull will not prevent you from moving upward the progressive movement of life currents and consciousness which you are trying to center in your divine Self (Figure 2).

Figure 2.

When To Meditate

Upon arising in the morning and the period just before retiring at night are the best for meditation. There are physiological reasons for choosing these periods. In the morning the body gets rid of poisons collected while sleeping and leave the body (through urination and other bodily excretions) when it awakens rendering your body calm, refresh, and more responsive to meditation; and at night, the body is relaxed and the life force can easily be withdrawn from the sensory nerves and the mind can simultaneously focus on uplifting endeavors.

Candle Lighting

Many people find it much easier to clear their mind when focusing on an open flame. Fire is hypnotic and can quickly transfix our thinking rendering our thoughts motionless. It is very effective in promoting meditation by simply staring at the candle flame. In this hypnotic state, the talking mind is subdued, and we can focus our attention on one thing at a time, or on nothing at all to allow our mind to go silent, be still.

Choose your candle carefully, aromatic or non-aromatic. Each serves a purpose. Aromas help raise your emotional nature while non-aromatic candles helps focus your mind. Their use depends on the goal at hand. That is to say, it is a good notion to have an assortment of aromatic and non-aromatic candles as part of your meditation practice. They have their own distinct force field conducting and redirecting energy that has gone awry. For instance, if you are feeling fearful or anxious, you may go into your meditation space, light up a Jasmine scented candle * and center your gaze on the flame. Then, focusing your attention on the fear or anxiety, mull over (for as long as you need) on what is causing those feelings, make up your mind to cut loose the thoughts causing the fear, and uplift your consciousness. Once outside your meditation space, relight the candle intermittently throughout the day or until you feel a lifting.

The aroma of the Jasmine is known for supporting relaxation, uplifting, soothing the nerves, removing negative influences, restoring mental clarity, optimism and energy, and bringing feelings of love and emotional warmth. The aroma emanating from the candle will create the supportive energy that can help disperse the negative emotions from your auric field. ** In addition, the energy of fear would have not only expressed itself in your auric field, but it would have also permeated your environment, and it could inadvertently be picked up again, even after your meditation. Continuing burning the aromatic candle *** can help you sustain the benefits of your meditation and keep you from unintentionally rekindling internal patterns of fear all over again.

A lighted candle in meditation practices is also used to symbolize the light of Truth in our human mind, the truth illuminating our soul's qualities, our faculties, and the Spirit of Love and Truth as the active principle dispelling ignorance and error. It symbolizes high spiritual aspirations drawing forth our higher states of consciousness in our innermost spiritual nature.

"The spirit of man is the candle of the Lord" (Proverb xx, 27). God being the fire of this world, the vital principle, the warm pervading presence everywhere, and the spirit of man is the candle.

Because we, Homo sapiens, are of the nature corresponding to the nature of God, the life of God gathers itself into utterance in us who He has kindled.

Note: Before lighting your candle, ascertain your meditation space is relatively dark or dimly lit, so that it is easy to hold your focus on the flame and maintain a relaxing, warm environment to aid your meditation. Keep the candle at about eye level to avoid straining your neck or slumping.

Incense Burning

You may burn incense moments before starting your meditation to enhance attunement. The calming effects of incense are well known by Monks, Nuns, and Spiritual Leaders. The ancients practiced using incense to set the mood for meditation. Certain aromatic incense can be used to slow down the heart rate and soothe the nerves. These calming effects help relieve built up tension in the muscles, enabling incense to not only be used as a muscle relaxer, but also to help induce a meditative state. It is a good way to help focus your attention and to purify your space for your meditation practice. In many cases, it can help you relieve stress and restore emotional balance.

There are many kinds of incense. Stick or cone incense is common.

The type of incense you choose depends upon your purpose. Intuitively, your Inner-Self will guide you to what is best for you. Still, if you are working toward a specific purpose you may desire to consider using some advocated scents.

Below are some choices

- For cleansing and purification: Sage. To cement the purification: Cedar.
- To clear and focus your mind, heighten intelligence, instill courage, restore mental clarity, promote calm and peace, and enhance your meditation: Frankincense, Jasmine, Lotus or Myrrh.
- To relief stress, promote beauty, attract love: Lavender or Rose.
- For grounding, balance, subdue aggression, irritability, and promote healing: Pine or Sandalwood.
- For energy, personal empowerment, and intelligence: Vanilla or Spice.
- To enhance psychic abilities, lift the spirit, purification: Anise, Frankincense, Lotus, or Myrrh.
- To induce dreams, peace of mind, financial blessings, sweetening thoughts, sharpen intuition, instill confidence: Honeysuckle, Jasmine, or Rosemary.
- To attract more positive things into your life, love, fertility, protection, defense, releasing: Patchouli.
- Seeking love, restoring balance and order, realigning one's energy, creating barriers and protection, removing negative influences: Experiment with Jasmine, Musk, or Rose.
- Goals related to prosperity, abundance, raising energy: Cinnamon, Sage, Clove, or Patchouli.

Incense fragrances and quality can vary. Some of them are subtle in their fragrances with less smoke. Others are more assertive and have more smoke. To a degree, practice safety.

SAFETY WARNINGS

Practice fire safety precautions with your candles and incense. Don't leave either unattended, especially with small children or animals in your house.

Use an incense holder or burner to burn your incense and a fireproof candleholder to hold your lighted candle.

"Trim the wick of your candle to ¼ inch each time before burning. Long or crooked wicks can cause uneven burning, dripping or flaring. Place the candleholder on a stable, heat-resistant surface. It will prevent possible heat damage to table surfaces and prevent glass containers from cracking or breaking. For a margin of safety, do not burn your candle all the way down. Discontinue burning a candle when 2 inches of wax remains (1/2 inch if in a container). Always keep the candle within your sight, and never burn a candle on or near anything that can catch fire. Do not blow out your candle. Use a candlesnuffer to extinguish it. It is the safest way to prevent hot wax from splattering. Do not use water to extinguish the candle. Water can cause the hot wax to splatter and might break a glass container. Ascertain the candle is completely out and the wick ember is no longer glowing before leaving your meditation space or the room where you lit your candle. Do not touch or move the candle until it has completely cooled. Never use a knife or sharp object to remove wax drippings from a glass holder. It might scratch, weaken or cause the glass to break upon subsequent use." (*National Candle Association*)

To extinguish burning incense, "break off the glowing tip and discard it in water or just dip the tip in water. If you use a censer, turn the stick upside down and bury the burning end in the sand or ash. The incense stick can then be relit in the future. For coil incense, you can break off the glowing tip and discard it in water" (*incensewarehouse.com*).

Some studies say that breathing incense smoke increases the risk of developing cancer, although it is much less perilous than smoking. Incense is not smoking and is not drawn directly into the lungs in the way tobacco smoke is, so the effect on the cells of the lungs may be very different. The study is just a reminder that burning anything—weather it is incense, coal or tobacco—produces smoke that can irritate and damage the lungs. All the same, you probably should not be breathing incense all day long. If incense causes irritation, you may choose to diffuse your surroundings with essential oils[1] of the same aroma as the incense you would choose for your meditation practice.

About Food

Ascertain there is no food in your stomach before meditation. In other words, do not eat before meditation. This is because life forces will be expended in digestion making it difficult to meditate. On the other hand, when you do eat, make sure your diet includes plenty of fruits and fresh vegetables. You secure nourishment when you incorporate their structures into your own body by eating them. This means that you gain control over the life force of the vegetables and fruits. Obtaining this control diverts the flow of their vital life force to it own uses harmonizing your body with the vital energy that is in them, which supplies the elements needed to overcome physical ailments. Ancient philosophy admits eating them alleviates suffering, and aids in the development of spiritual, mental, moral, or physical powers.

POSTURE

The body and the mind are interlinked. They impact each other. The posture you take can support or interfere with concentration. The optimal posture is seated, without reclining, yet relaxed (without strain or tension).

Correct posture is an avenue to help the mind be attentive and constant. Being seated and keeping your back straight is conducive to meditation, just like lying down is conducive to help you fall asleep. In like manner, the positions of your feet, hands, gaze, etc. are all techniques that take advantage of means to influence the mind and the body.

The object is to direct your mind and the life force upward through the spine and into the centers of higher consciousness in the brain. The legs can be kept slightly apart with feet flat on the ground (resting on top of a wool blanket or silk cloth) and hands placed upward or downward on your lap unclasped.

If you experience difficulty in maintaining the erect position make the necessary adjustments to fit your specific need, but always aim toward accomplishing the optimal posture.

Ascertain there are no restrictions around your body when you sit to meditate. Clothing should be loose and any dangling object from the body should be removed. Wearing heavy earrings, for example, can be a distraction, as is wearing tight clothing. They cause physical discomfort making concentration difficult.

---

*   A white candle can be used if you cannot find the aroma or color candle you desire.

** **Auric field**—Subtle bodies (Etheric, Astral, Emotional, Mental, Soul/Causal, Buddhic, Atmic) corresponding to subtle plane of existences that culminates in the physical form. They create an interconnecting field of energy around the physical body. Each subtle body connects into the physical body via a psychic center or chakra—center of spiritual power in the human body—, which directs the energy into the physical body via the meridian system, a set of pathways associated with specific organs.

Meridians provide the transport service for the fundamental substances of qi (the circulating life force), blood, and body fluids. The flow of qi in the Meridian System concentrates or "injects" in certain areas of the skin's surface (See Figure 1 below).

Chakras are the centers in our bodies in which energy flows through. Chakra is an old Sanskrit word that literally translates to wheel. This spinning energy has 7 centers in our bodies, starting at the base of our spine and moving all the way up to the top of our head (See Figure 2 below).

*** A list of various aromas and their benefits is given in the incense burning section.

[1]   Essential oils are concentrated versions of natural oils typically obtained by distillation and having the characteristic fragrances of the plants or other sources from which they are extracted (plant roots, leaves stems, flowers, or bark).

Sources:

Crystalherbs.com
Google's dictionary
Mindvalley.com
Wikipedia

Figure 1

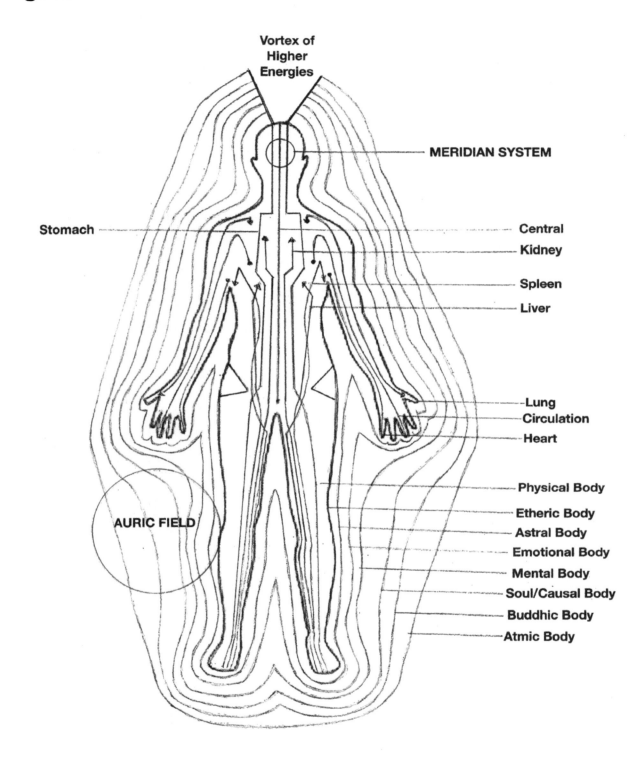

Figure 2

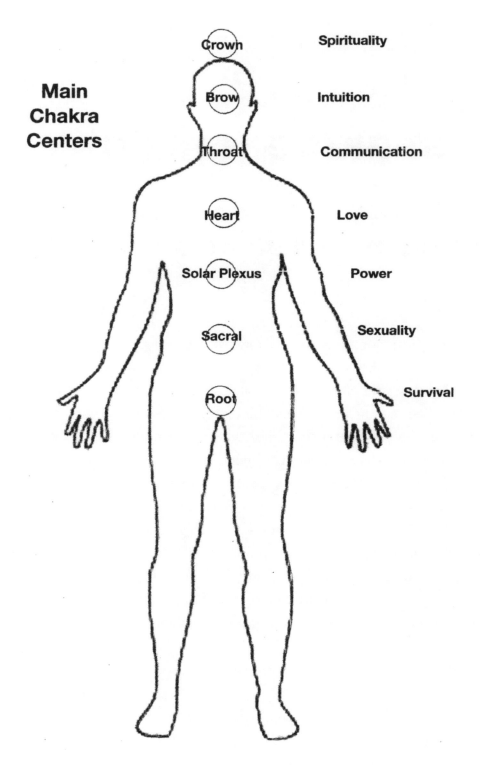

6

SEEKING HARMONY

MEDITATION BY OBSERVATION

Practical Application

Viewing life without disguises allows you to inwardly observe the ceaseless waves of emotions and thoughts that arise within you as you begin to analyze the source of your yearnings, the nature of your endeavors, your ideals, hopes, and despairs. You discover that from your emotions (the feelings enthralled in your heart) arise thought and response, that faster than thought, is the response that originates from feeling, and that to retain control over the observation, you must view the thought and the response as a spectator.

You find that your yearnings, endeavors, ideals, hopes, and despairs demand that you use your intelligence, wisdom, love, and vision to understand that life is manifesting itself trough these mediums; that life is naught if it is not a progressive overcoming of problems; that each problem anticipates a solution held at hand and imposed upon you by life itself; that any fleeing from problems, physical or mental is fleeing from life, as there can be no life that is not brimful of problems. Mostly, you learn that conditions are neutral, seeming to be either discouraging or encouraging depending on the pessimistic or optimistic mental outlook of the mind concerned with them.

So, it rests with you to climb above the state of affairs in your life, to wake up your quintessence, honesty, self-control, and desire for good things, and to wage furious battle to maintain inner peace. Sorrows do not emerge out of the conditions of life; they are not inborn in the conditions. They are built-in in the frail and infirm characteristics of Homo sapiens, us.

You find that by heeding the lessons that accompany affliction and happiness, you avoid the actions that cause affliction and follow the ways that lead to enjoyment, satisfaction, jubilation, and happiness.

Deeply, joyously, and continuously practice meditation by inner observation to reach your destination, which is to find truth. Record your findings for easy view and contemplation of the lessons learned. Once you have awakened your higher consciousness, it will tell you all that you need to know. The depth of calmness and concentration necessary for this are easily developed through the regular practice of meditation.

7

EXPANDING AWARENESS

MEDITATION BY METHODICAL EXPERIMENTATION

Practical Application

We become aware when we are in a state of knowing, of being informed about, conscious of, mindful of, acquainted with, familiar with, alive to, and alert to. Unless we become aware of situations that influence us adversely, we cannot realize true spiritual success. Our attention would be scattered and/or focused on the problem at hand versus devising ways to solve the problem, which would help us gain entrance into higher consciousness. Let us consider stress.

Stress stems in consciousness. Stress – our body's state of alarm – is a measure of our reaction to our surroundings reflecting how we are not coping. To some, it is a crisis of values, meaning, and purpose; to others, it is a provocation to learn and grow. So, what is it that rules our reactions to potentially stressful situations? What is it that ushers right action, poise, and minimum stress in life?

SABOTAGING ONESELF

Have you ever had a gut feeling before you did something that it was not in your best interest to do, but ignored that feeling and went ahead and did it anyway, and as a consequence, intensified the pain and turmoil in your life?

We all have a built-in sensing mechanism (fight or flight) that when correctly used, lights the way for our actions in life. Just by virtue of being born human, we are endowed with higher faculties of consciousness that are capable of giving us facts relevant to our worldly undertakings and realistic-intuitive input, which our rationalizing mind is not equipped to manage. We speak of having a gut feeling, a hunch, or feeling it in our bones. These are all verbalizations of instinctive feedback signals we are not picking up. Our higher mind is necessarily attempting to project to our rational awareness some consequential aspect of reality that might otherwise go unnoticed by relying solely on the rational mind.

If you are experiencing stress or burnout symptoms, you have also probably overruled your own inner knowing, disregarded some essential feedback signal from your inner self, soul, or nature which knows without taking thought. You find that by attuning to the ongoing inner guidance of your own higher consciousness, stress, as most men and women perceive it, ceases to exist.

One way of attuning to this higher consciousness is by exploring and experimenting with energy patterns that create and unify all things and reveals the precise way that the energy of creation organizes itself in your human body. You'll see that in each case, every natural pattern of growth or movement adheres to one or more geometric shapes.

INTUITIVE INPUT AND METHODICAL EXPERIMENTATION

"Ponder all things, and establish high thy mind."

Pythagoras

For centuries mystics have known that by meditating and experimenting on special geometric designs one can have a mesmerizing effect that results in the expansion of our awareness. Geometry is an expression of energy, a significant force conditioning human consciousness and essential to the education of our soul. Geometry is symbolic of our own inner realm and the subtle structure of knowing. Consider the circle for example. It is symbolical of the "all-embracing principle of divine manifestation, perfect and entire, including everything and wanting nothing, without beginning or end, neither first nor last, time-less, sex-less, absolute." (*Dictionary Of Scriptures And Myths*, 158). Consider also the intricate symmetry, the beauty and balance of geometric proportions, as it exists in man. Man has within himself all what is reflected in our universe—the best and most harmonious proportions of being. Your human body contains in its proportions all the important geometric geodesic measures and functions. This can be seen in the Vitruvian Man drawn by Leonardo Da Vinci.[1]

Contemplating and experimenting with geometry allows you to focus directly at the forms representing the physiognomy of intelligence and offers up a glance into the inner workings of the Universal Mind of which you are a part.

With basic geometric expressions in Nature and in Man that can in some way influence our consciousness, the ancients created overpasses—Yantras and Mandalas—to an intuitive spiritual understanding that is in alignment with the appropriate use of this knowledge. Yantras and Mandalas are geometric designs having profound effect on our psyche and we can use them to methodically experiment and settle ourselves into a higher or heightened state of awareness.

YANTRAS

Literally, a *Yantra* is a loom, an instrument or machine. Machines are instrumental. They are molded into a combination of purposeful forms to render service. For example, if you like to beat an egg, you reach for a fork or a whisk – a yantra. You can probably use your fingers to beat the egg, but this purposeful form (the fork) or yantra lets you use your body in a more efficient way. Even though you already have the body – the most sophisticated yantra – with you, it is possible to carry out different functions better with specific machines for those functions.

Yantras are instruments to improve your life in different capacities. You can make them for specific purposes, and different types of yantras carry their own vibration. Considering the kind of energy you desire to create, you can make that kind of yantra. The most primitive yantra is a simple triangle. A triangle with the point facing upward is one kind of yantra; with the point facing downward, is another kind. You can mix them in many different ways and make an array of yantras.

Anything you do, you can excel with the help of a yantra. It is a powerful, personalized instrument that creates a certain field and an ambience so that your welfare is inherently taken care of. It is for busy people who are always on the go, actively pursuing businesses, careers and family life, and who desire to do many things.

A yantra being a machine must do work, function and deliver a product. Every machine is essentially only an adjunct of a faculty that you already have. You can run, but with a car you can mobilize much faster and go further. You can handwrite, but with a typewriter you can write much faster. Yantras are designed to achieve definitive purposes and bring about certain pursuits or abilities.

Symbolically, a yantra is a mystical diagram that represents aspects of the Divine. That is, yantras are also referred to as the abodes of the divine powers of God. It is made of interlocking

geometric figures, circles, triangles, floral shapes that form a pattern, and many other geometric forms found in Nature and in Man. They are energized with mantras[2] that sometimes are seen written in the design. Mantras are generators of specific currents of sublime sound and their perceivable manifestation. Thus, a *Yantra* is a monogram[3]—a spectrograph[4] of this sonic energy. It is a visual mantra, a verbal repetition (usually a positive affirmation in a geometric form) used as an object to direct your mind in concentration and meditation. It is a device created through the ages by mystics to aid humanity in its quest for wellbeing and as a support system toward a particular goal.

Generally, yantras are engraved on copper or silver plates. Presently, you can also see them in multi-colored inks on paper. In terms of their spiritual effects, yantras are like schematic sketches of the anatomy of divine energy fields. Keeping them in a particular direction in the house, and concentration upon them it is said to have noticeable encouraging results. Each yantra needs to be installed with the use of particular mantras.

ANATOMY OF YANTRAS

A dot (.) in the cryptographs (coded messages) of yantras represents absoluteness and completeness in potentiality (realm of infinite possibilities). It is an emblem of the core of cosmic energy and hence stands for the power-source of all activities and motion of the phenomenon of nature in the universe. Spiritually, it implicates pure knowledge, understanding, and ultimate awareness. The extensions of a dot in circular patterns, in a yantra, are associated mien in varied forms. Connecting three dots results in a triangle. Contrasting lengths of the straight lines joining the dots, contrasting angles between them, and the contrasting triangular and other shapes generated by that together with free dots, circles, straight, curvilinear, convergent, and divergent lines are the fundamental ingredients that makeup a yantra, and yet, imagination also plays a part. Make your yantra to fit your needs.

MAKING YOUR YANTRA

Specific configurations can be incorporated in your yantras to invoke potencies and thereby awake higher powers within your mind and consciousness to lead to a thorough self-knowledge. Begin by selecting a coding system of symbols, signs, alphabets and digits to represent the syllables of your mantra(s) associated with your natural tendencies of consciousness, emotional impulses, your constitution and bodily health, your mind, your potentialities and weaknesses, your experiences. Add to these, the influence of your parents, education, environment, and the five elements—fire, air, water, earth, ether; that is, the ether of space, the fiery, gaseous, liquid and solid states of matter. Why should we consider adding the five elements of matter? It is because they are governed by cosmic intelligences, which work through much lower intelligences governing man (*The Secret Teachings Of All Ages*, LVIII). The five elements are not detached; rather they work closely together and have their own interior arrangements and patterns affecting you in unseen ways. The meaning of the five elements together with their symbols gives you a comprehensive understanding of how you, as a human being, are both physically and mentally intertwined with nature and how you can use this knowledge for your benefit.

THE FIVE ELEMENTS AND THEIR SYMBOLS

I

<u>Symbols</u>: **Ether of Space**

<u>Meaning</u>: The medium, which holds all the other elements together, which fills space and intervenes between the realms of vital energy and organic and inorganic substances—works through our throat center.

<u>Benefits</u>: Regulates the anatomical regions of the thyroid, parathyroid, jaw, neck, mouth, tongue, and larynx and helps us to speak, listen, express ourselves from a higher form of communication, and to hear the subtle aspect of sound.

II

Symbols: **Air Element**

Meaning: Symbolically, it represents "Mind" (*Dictionary Of All Scriptures And Myths*, 35)—works through our heart center.

Benefits: Regulates our heart, cardiac plexus, thymus gland, lungs, breasts, and lymphatic system. When this center is open, it helps us flow through life with love and compassion, helps us breathe better, and sense the subtle world.

Blockages: When this center is closed, it gives way to grief, anger, jealousy, and fear of betrayal, self-hatred and hatred toward others.

III

Symbols: **Fire Element**

Meaning: Swift energy and penetrating power, which cleanses and transforms (Ibid. 276)—works around the navel in the area of the solar plexus and up to the breastbone.

Benefits: Regulates our metabolism, digestion, and cognitive processes. This center is used to increase personal power, to govern self-esteem, warrior energy, and the power of transformation. It is related to motivation, creativity, and passion.

Blockages: Over excitation or too much fire can be detrimental because no limits are enforced, leaving the individual exhausted and off balance leading to selfishness, egocentricity, and unrealistic expectations of others. Too little fire leads to low energy and a lack of motivation.

IV

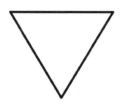

Symbols: **Water Element**

Meaning: Source of all manifestation. Cohesiveness—works through the sacral center.

Benefits: Regulates our emotions and helps us feel wellness, abundance, pleasure, and joy.

Blockages: When this center is out of balance, emotional instability, fear of change, sexual dysfunction, depression, or addictions may be experienced. You may open this center with creative expressions (play like a child) and by honoring your body.

V

Symbols: **Earth Element**

Meaning: Symbolically, it is the lower nature of the soul—lower mental, astral, and physical planes, which constitute the arena of life for the ego (Ibid. 237)—works through the base center (located at the base of the spine, the pelvic floor, and the first three ascending vertebrae).

Benefits: Helps us keep our physical tissues in a good state. It governs money, property, business, loyalty, responsibility, our sense of safety and security on this earthly journey, and our emotional needs, such as letting go of fear.

Blockages: An over abundance of this element slows things down and progress is slow; and too little of this element causes an inability to dare, take risks or branch out.

DEVISING A YANTRA TO INCLUDE THE 5 ELEMENTS

Let us say you may long to have robust health and wish to draw a yantra that represents your desire to have the five elements governing your being in the correct proportions to achieve physical, emotional, and mental wellness. Your desire is to boost your overall health understanding that in order to achieve complete wellness, the spirit, mind and body all need to be in harmony. You then focus on increasing your spiritual health to have a positive effect on your physical health. You desire to get to know your spirit, to bring out your true emotions, to meditate and de-stress, look at things positively, refuel your spirit, and discover who you really are. A yantra portraying the 5 elements in you can be drawn to represent these desires.

Draw a human form with the symbols of the 5 elements in it. Knowing the different organs they govern, you can place them accordingly in the human form, and thus make a visual representation that defines robust health in your mind's eye. Add to this, a positive statement or a mantra.

Following are some affirmations or mantras that can be said or held in consciousness to replace the existing energy, changing it to another form to facilitate healing, hence, robust health.

- Spirit is renewing me now.
- I am willing to accept my life right now and choose robust health today.
- I accept God's healing grace to heal my body.
- I am renewed by love.
- I treasure my body as the temple of my soul.
- I choose whole, healthy means in every area of my life.
- I am healthy and functioning in God's world as part of his grand spiritual plan.
- My being is flooded with the spirit of love, life, and health.
- I stop throughout the day to breathe deep to optimize my health.
- I forgive myself for my past history.
- I forgive others for participating in my learning.
- I create my life purpose and a specific plan for how to achieve it.
- I fill my life with laughter, play, and fun.
- I am eating healthy today.
- I claim peace deep within.
- Every part of my body is in conformity with the living Spirit within me.
- I know that this day in which I live, this present time, which is now, is flawless.
- My body is a habitat of the living Spirit.

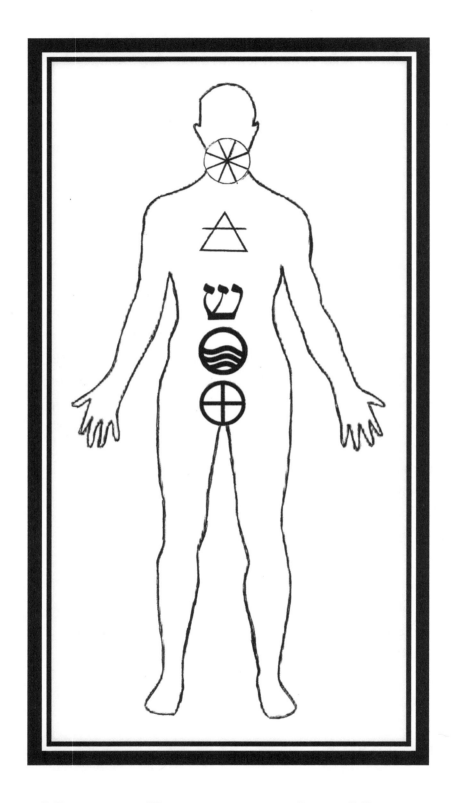

**Yantra Representing Your
True health potential**

The mind being the faculty of consciousness and thought can be included to add power to your yantra and send a powerful message of health to your subconscious mind. This may be represented by a triangle hovering to the right and above the human form.

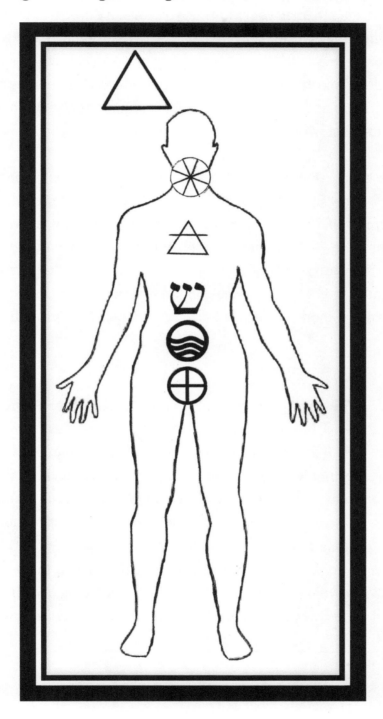

Yantra Reflecting Your Mind over Matter/Body

EXPERIMENTING WITH SYMBOLS

Pick your symbols. Working with them will allow their meaning and energy into your consciousness. By including them in your yantras, you can have access to the energy and meaning that comes from your inner world: that is, from your emotional reactions, your ideas, your fantasies, imagination or dreams. They communicate more directly than words. Figuratively, it is an object representing another. They give an entirely different meaning that is much deeper and more significant. Ideas and qualities are symbolized making the symbols more effective by given you a visual picture of what you are trying to convey in your yantra. Meaning and emotion are brought forth.

Symbols are like a shorthand method of representing the phenomenon of existence. For example, instead of writing out the name of an element, you can represent the element's name with one or two letters, such as the element "water" or H_2O. Or, you can use the symbols of numerals for numbers, the yin and yang symbols for the female/male principle, solstices' and equinoxes' symbols for your spiritual awakening, and so forth. The use of objects, seasons, people, situations, and words are all types of symbolism that can be used in your yantra.

Following are two common symbols utilized in yantras to portray distinctive features or dominant ideas.

Yin-Yang

Female & Male

The Yin-Yang Symbol / Female and Male Principle. Yin, the dark swirl, is associated with the female principle of all generation and Yang, the light swirl, represents the male principle, the dynamic, replete, and fecundating force. Their attraction and union keep your mind active and in motion. Yang is rendered as intellect and it is that which urges and moves your mind to make decisions. It gives direction to your existence. Yin is rendered as will and it is used to bring forth the conceptions of your mind. It is your mind's volitive faculty, the dynamo that feeds all powers of your mind, initiating and keeping in continuous operation all activities of your mind (*Universal Mind Revealed*, 15, 16, 17).

The OM or AUM Symbol. This symbol is an expression of the Spirit as Love within the soul; or the Word of God—the inspiration of Truth and Righteousness (*Dictionary Of All Scriptures and Myths*, 550). It is the Holy Spirit: the invisible divine power, the only doer, the sole causative and activating force that upholds all creation through vibration. It is the blissful Comforter revealing the meditator the ultimate Truth, bringing all things to remembrance.

DEVISING A YANTRA TO INCLUDE THE YIN-YANG AND AUM SYMBOLS

Let us say that you are interested in making a yantra to represent three things: 1) your mind's ability to devise strategies or plans of action to achieve a major aim. 2) your volitive faculty becoming dynamic enough to actively pursue your plans; and 3) the Spirit of God governing its outcome. Let us say you choose the Yin-Yang and the AUM symbols to stand for the male aspect of your mind conceptualizing your plans, your female aspect willing and acting until victory is attained, and the immaterial part of you (your soul) stimulating your creativity to bring forth your heart's desire. Let us also say, you choose a short, powerful statement as a mantra to inspire and motivate you into action and to aid your concentration in the production of spiritual efficacy effecting your will to act on your plans.

Draw your yantra showing both, the Yin-Yang and AUM symbols to effectively influence your thinking and write a mantra that would say, for example: "I am calm, resourceful and ready to go forward." Thus, one yantra (Figure 1) may contain the Yin-Yang in full view showing the interaction of the male and female principles at work, being fruitful, diligently pursuing your goal, and your soul embedded in each encouraging every step of the way, while another yantra (Figure 2) may have the AUM symbol in full view showing the sole causative and activating force of the male/female principle pursuing your idea, your creation. Add a mantra glorifying God for bringing your desires to fruition. Thus, your mantra may say, for example: "My creator now blesses me with perfect acceptance and confidence in my own ability to achieve."

Figure 1   **Figure 2**

DEVISING A YANTRA TO INCLUDE SOLSTICES' AND EQUINOXES' SYMBOLS

No matter where you are in the world, people recognize Solstices, Equinoxes and their corresponding symbols. It is this instant recognition that makes symbology invaluable. All the meaning behind them, all the associations that come with them, give people an understanding without explanation. They will know what to expect without having to think about it.

In simple terms, an *equinox* represents a day with equal duration of day and night (March 21st and September 22nd) and thus we have a spring and a fall *equinox*.

Solstice refers to a day with either the longest day (June 21st, also called summer *solstice*) or shortest day (December 21st, also referred to as winter *solstice*).

Spiritually, the solstices and equinoxes are to do with the journey and transitions of the sun. The sun represents the Son in us—a universal and personal spiritual force that has been enacted by enlightened beings throughout time, such as Buddha, Jesus, and others, and by the sun and stars in their movements in relation to the earth every year. The universe reveals this process of spiritual awakening to mankind each year. It is said that the outer drama enacted in the heavens is actually an inner portrayal of us becoming spiritual, with the sun representing the spiritual aspect that incarnates within each of us.

Knowing the meaning and corresponding symbols for each of the solstices and equinoxes may have a strong effect in you, hence, on your yantras.

Vernal or Spring Equinox Symbology. The year always begins with the Vernal Equinox celebrating March 21st to mark the moment when the sun crosses the equator northward up the zodiacal arc, making night and day of approximately equal length all over the earth.

The Vernal Equinox is said to occur in the constellation of Aries (the Ram). In ancient times, this constellation was called the "Lamb of God" and the "Savior," and was said to save mankind from its sins. Devotees made up prayers, much like mantras, often repeating the words, "O Lamb of God, that takes away the sins of the world, have mercy upon us. Grant us Thy peace." The Lamb of God is a title given to the sun, which is said to be reborn every year in the Northern Hemisphere in the sign of the Ram (*The Secret Teachings Of All Ages*, LIV), spiritually denoting the mysteries of spiritual resurrection. It is a time of great confrontation between the forces of darkness and light. It symbolizes what an initiate[5] goes through while in the decisively and paramount stage of self-realization, where the struggle between darkness and light produces the hurdles necessary to obtain immortality.

To represent the symbology of the Vernal Equinox, you may devise a yantra that can denote the spiritual resurrection you are seeking and the hurdles to be surmounted to obtain life eternal. In the following example, the "ankh" is used to represent life eternal, the stairs to represent the "hurtles" to be surmounted, and the "Lamb of God" (the Ram) to represent your determination to climb to the top.

"I am triumphant in all my undertakings" is a good mantra that can be used to strengthen your yantra.

Summer Solstice Symbology. The Solstice marks the onset of summer at the time of the longest day, about June 21th in the northern hemisphere, at which time, the sun proceeds to descend the zodiacal arc. It reminds us that the season is short, slipping away day by day.

The Summer Solstice is regarded as occurring in Cancer (the Crab), which the Egyptians called the *scarab*—a beetle of the family Lamellicornes, the head of the insect kingdom, and sacred to the Egyptians as the symbol of Eternal Life.

"Cancer is the symbol of generation, for it is the house of the Moon, the great Mother of all things and the patroness of the life forces of Nature. The Crab has the property of spontaneously detaching from its own body any limb that has been hurt or mutilated, and reproduces another in its place" (Ibid. LIV). You can use this property of crabs as an instrument of spiritual teaching to symbolize the return and ascension to the kingdoms of God celebrating the triumph of light over darkness and the return to wholeness, one great-unified consciousness supported by a complete, whole, and powerful luminescence that lights your way.

Light being a symbol of Truth, Wisdom and Knowledge, and of the consciousness apprehends reality or relativity in each (*Dictionary Of All Scriptures And Myths*, 451). That is to say, awareness allows your consciousness to apprehend facts or perspectives in Truth, Wisdom and Knowledge when they are presented for consideration.

TRIUMPH OF LIGHT OVER DARKNESS

Here you are, at the pinnacle of the solar year and the Sun is at the apex of its life-giving power, a time of joy, expansiveness, and the celebration of achievements. Being an important moment on your spiritual cycle, you can align the element of fire, passion, will and drive to seek right action, to choose to walk in alignment with your convictions, and to look at the grander scope of your life and spiritual path. A yantra representing the Summer Solstice will give you an aperture into the personal power you can cultivate and manifest as a new habit, a new relationship, a new way of dealing with yourself, relaxing, letting go, letting things reach their fullness without the striving of the ego, letting nature take its course, and giving thanks to the Divine Sun, which you can hold in your hand to light your way. The following yantra depicts this representation—attainments reached and the ability to take power from above and direct it through desire into manifestation.

In this next example, the rock is used to represent steadfastness, the eternal, and the permanent, the long-lasting element of the physical world enabling you to be more productive and more efficient as when rocks were used as tools and weapons to survive in the stone-age, and in present days, to build superstructures, altars and the like.

The man standing on the rock is used to represent you building all things on a strong, firm foundation and being sheltered from adversity.

The man holding the Sun is used to represent your Higher Self, the central source of Light and Life within your soul guiding your way, being triumphant.

Make up mantras to strengthen your Summer Solstice's yantra. Some examples are listed below:

- I conclude all matters in plenty, perfection and gayety.
- Happy issues, liberality, and abundance are mine.
- Happy family life, true friendships, lasting success, happiness and attainment of my heart's desires are mine.
- I rest from strife and retreat into solitude to receive good advice, counsel, and instruction from my soul.
- I accept freedom, relaxation from fear, and harmony in the midst of change.
- I am prudent in using all my powers to make the right choices.

Autumnal Equinox Symbology. The Autumnal Equinox takes place on or about September 22nd in the northern hemisphere.

The Autumnal Equinox is said to occur in the constellation of Libra (the Balances). The scales tip and the solar globe begins its pilgrimage toward the house of winter crossing the plane of earth's equator and making night and day approximately equal in length.

"The constellation of the Scales was placed in the zodiac to symbolize the power of choice, by means of which man may weigh one problem against another" (*The Secret Teachings Of All Ages*, LIV). From our emotional reactions to our environment we distill the product of experience, which then aids us to regain our lost position (before we knew good and evil) plus an individualized intelligence.

The autumn equinox is interlaced with the two solstices (winter and summer), and the spring equinox to mark stages in our mystical work that begins anew each year, and forms a symbolic cross in the "wheel of the year",[6] with the sun—the spiritual aspect that incarnates within us—at the center.

THE POWER OF CHOICE

Change can pose a hefty challenge to an individual's endurance. But, each change is a single step along a spiritual journey, a spiritual transformation that mirrors endings, a very natural thing, for every journey must find its end and the Autumnal Equinox is the bittersweet embodiment of this.

There comes a time when change must be faced, including autumn descent into one's own inner darkness. Darkness exists in all of us—we are flawed, imperfect mortals. Darkness, ignored, advances and takes over like a malignant tumor—it is only when it is hauled into the light that we can defeat it. Autumn is the time to confront this darkness, and it is a physical reminder of that which we must slaughter within ourselves.

At the same time, autumn is a time of concurrent bounty and withering; crops are harvested, even as leaves fall from trees and wither.

Consider the things in your life that need to go, which no longer serve you, get in your way of progress and need to wither. Consider also the germs of thoughts, ideals, and desires that you cultivated in your mind at the beginning of the year, and that have been firmly flourishing. Allow those germs of thoughts, ideals, and desires—that bountiful harvest—to be reaped.

Make a yantra to represent the Autumnal Equinox, with the scale at its midst weighing your mind and heart against the interrelated and eternally consistent harmony of nature, with truth in one side of the scale and fairness in the other, comparing what you offer to the world and what is received, your inherent values and distributed goodness, your understanding at the point of equilibrium and assertion that your truth is not crucified in the middle of two contradictory or conflicting concepts of ideals; a yantra that represents changes to be faced, the eradication of darkness from your life, levelness or evenness of mind, making decisions by weighing one problem against another in a fair manner, and the harvest of germ thoughts, ideals, and desires.

In the following yantra the Lady Justice is used to personify moral force slaughtering darkness (withered leaves) with a sword—a symbol of power and protection. The sword also stands for authority to make decisions, which aids in the selection of a course of action among several alternatives. Further, it stands for strength and courage, beneficial qualities that increases the chances of success or effectiveness in purging, typically giving a sense of cathartic release. Moreover, it stands for discrimination and the penetrating power of the intellect. Discrimination allows one to recognize and understand the difference between one thing and another and the power of intellect gives the capacity to understand objectively, especially with regard to abstract thinking.

The blindfold is used to represents objectivity in slaughtering darkness, meted out dispassionately, without fear or benevolence.

The scale is used to represent inner balance, righteousness, order, impartial decision making, free of whims and prejudice, weighing evidence of support or opposition in given situations, punishment and mercy, and seeking balance to enable steadiness.

The bountiful harvest represents the germs thoughts, ideals, and desires that have been reaped.

Mantras

Sacred utterances, numinous sounds, syllables, and grouped words added to your yantra can have psychological and spiritual powers. They help penetrate the depths of the unconscious mind and adjust the vibration of all aspects of your being. Here are some examples:

- I am perfect understanding.
- I triumph in all undertakings.
- I accept change of position and renewal.
- I change in personal consciousness, which is now blending with the universal.
- I know that inspiration and guidance are mine.
- I am harmonious within and without.
- My trials are done and I am now whole.
- I accept perfect order.
- Infinite wisdom now guides me.
- I release the shadow; I accept the light.
- Illusion passes; love remains.
- There is a right solution for everything, and I know it now.
- The power of God now leads me out of the valley of the shadow of death into the light of truth and freedom.

Winter Solstice Symbology. At the Winter Solstice, on or about December 21st, the northern hemisphere is leaning most away from the sun for the year. Earth is positioned in its orbit so that the sun stays below the North Pole horizon.

"The constellation of Capricorn, in which the Winter Solstice takes place, was called *The House of Death*, for in winter all life in the northern hemisphere is at its lowest ebb. Capricorn is a composite creature, with the head and upper body of a goat and the tail of a fish. In this constellation the sun is least powerful in the northern hemisphere" (Ibid. LIV) and after passing through this constellation its power immediately begins to increase reaching its full strength at the summer solstice.

The constellation Capricorn is regarded as a doorway into life of those who know not death, those whose will arrive at fulfillment and the envisioned goal is reached. Man reaches either the height of personal ambition or becomes the initiate, attaining spiritual awareness. The initiate becomes aware of the growing light, which meets his progress as he climbs upward to the summit. The glint of intuition with which he is becoming familiar changes into the flaming and continual light of the soul, illuminating his mind and producing a junction between the lesser and the greater light within, blending the light of his personality and that of his soul.

The winter solstice is a celebration of being "born again"— the dying of the old and the making way for the new. It is a celebration of the birth of the spiritual Self within our consciousness transforming us completely from inner darkness into the light of our soul.

During this time, we are reminded to take a look into the deepest aspects of our inner nature, to realign our choices to the greatest of intentions for what the New Year will bring and make progress in our journey of awakening. Devise a yantra to symbolize this.

In the following example, the Capricorn composite creature is used to represent the doorway into an exalted state of mind (the mountain) where the divine plan may be perceived and unfolded, a state of spiritual realization.

The high mountain to which your personality (the doorway) carries you in your spiritual rousing is used to represent the consciousness of power over mortal thought in all its physical channels of expression. It represents the aspiration towards ideals, the rise of the soul to higher planes of consciousness.

The valley of trees is used to represent the soul's aspirations to bring forth deeds bearing fruit.

Your threefold nature—consisting of your physical organism, your emotional nature, and your mental faculties and represented by the upright triangle rising beyond the mountain—reflect the light of your threefold Divinity and the bearing witness of it in the physical world. If the upright triangle is seen as a pyramid, it can represent reaching into higher realms of consciousness to cleanse, purify, and balance your body's electromagnetic field to deliver healing at all levels.

The Sun rising is used to represent the Higher Self—the central source of Light, and Life within your soul meeting your progress as you climb to the summit.

Adding concise and forceful expressive utterances (Mantras) can be used to invigorate your yantra.

Mantras

- I am perfect attainment, ecstasy, felicity, bliss, prosperity, and wealth.
- I penetrate matter and influence it with my thoughts.
- New beginnings are now possible.
- My soul guides me, counsels me, and instructs me.
- I advance as my soul advances.
- I attain my heart's desires.
- All creation turns to me for my final development.
- I accept my spiritual perfection and triumph in all undertakings.
- Within me is the urge to unfold my highest potential—to feel again my native joy, limitless freedom, and omnipotence.
- Daily, I resurrect myself from the illusion of being a helpless victim of the ever-changing dualities of this world.
- I gain a sense of freedom by resurrecting the power of my will from passive submission to the ego's impulses.
- I choose my course in each situation by soul-wisdom.

MANDALAS

Literally, a *Mandala* is a geometric figure, a "circle" representing the universe in Hindu and Buddhist symbolism. In common use, "*Mandala*" has become a generic term for any diagram, chart or geometric pattern that represents the cosmos metaphysically or symbolically, a microcosm of the universe. It is viewed as sacred, allowing the meditator to settle into a higher or heightened state of awareness. In clinical setups it has been used to boost the immune system, reduce stress and pain, lower blood pressure, promote sleep and ease depression.

Mandala artwork has a long history and is recognized for its deep spiritual meaning, representation of wholeness, and a meaningful reflection of its creator, you!

Mandala artwork can be a great source of reflection on your soul. It has one identifiable center point, from which emanates an array of symbols, shapes and geometric and organic forms.

The scope of personal benefits from making a *Mandala* encompasses from quieting the emotions to physical health, from mental clarity to spiritual growth. It promotes greater awareness of self and life, creates satisfaction and pleasure, helps overcome blocks and stuck patterns in daily living, makes meditation easier and more accessible, grounds and centers your consciousness, integrates polarities within yourself (yin-yang ☯), increases concentration, stimulates your creative thinking and problem-solving capabilities, accesses your "Master" within, aligns your body, emotions, mind, and soul, opens your heart chakra, assists you in reaching your full potential, and promotes your spiritual enlightenment.

DRAWING A MANDALA

Supplies needed:

A pencil, pen, or any other drawing instrument you prefer

A drawing surface to accommodate the size of the Mandala you desire to make

A ruler or protractor

A compass or any circular objects that you can trace

Drawing Steps

1. **With your compass, draw a large circle on your drawing surface; this will be the size of your Mandala. If you do not have a compass, you can trace the circle around an object such as a plate, the rim of a drinking glass, or draw it freehand.**

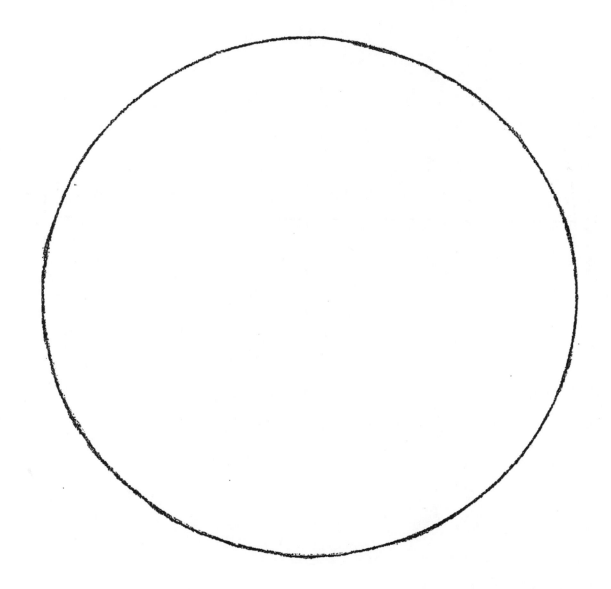

2. **With your ruler, draw one line horizontally in the center of your circle, then another vertically, so that you have four equal quadrants in the circle.**

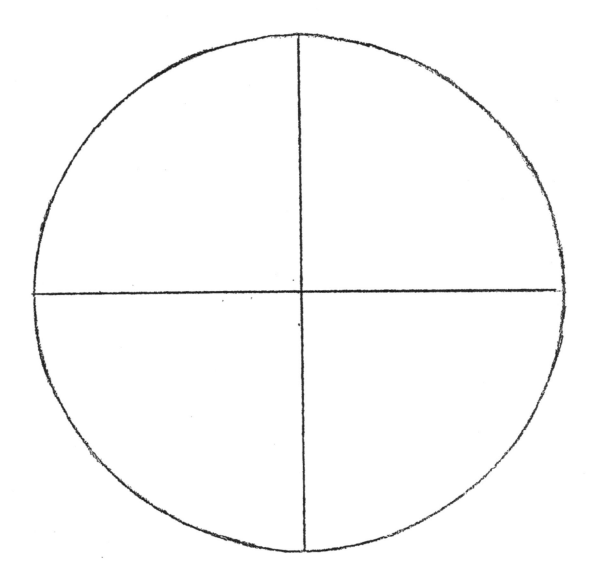

3. **Start your array of symbols, geometric shapes, and organic forms by drawing a small circle in the center of your large circle.**

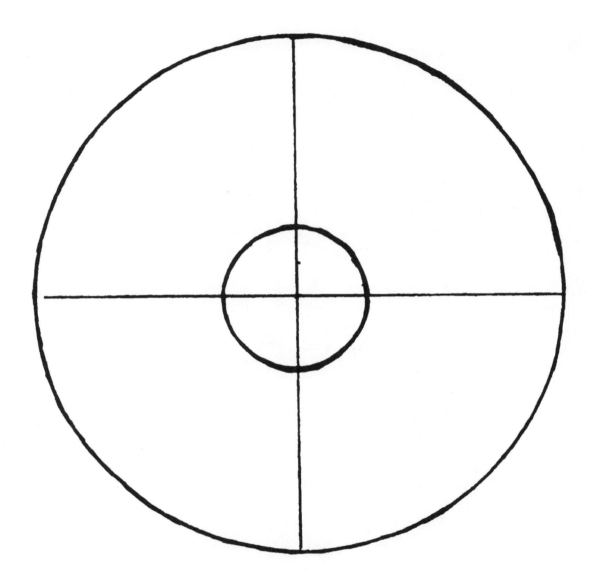

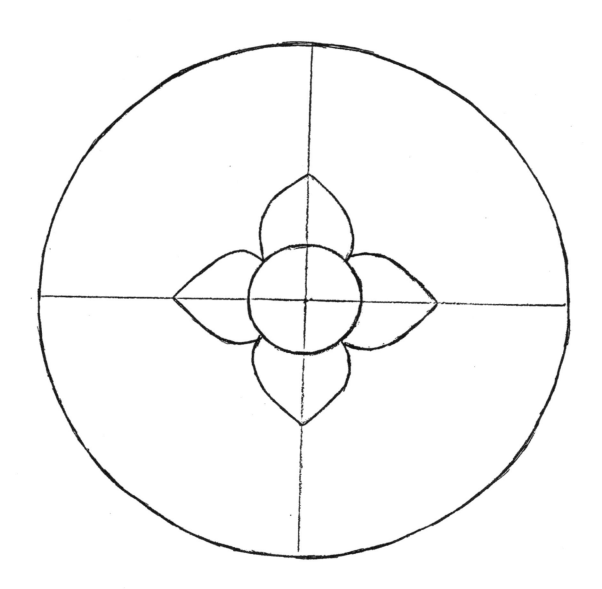

4. **Create your organic shapes (i.e.: flower petals, etc.) coming out of each of the four quadrants from the small circle.**

5. **Working from the "negative" spaces (spaces around the petals or any other organic forms you chose to draw around the small circle) in your current design, draw additional shapes. These can be a new shape or the same shapes you initially drew at a different height. Build your way out from the central figure. Maintain a uniform and symmetrical arrangement. Make additional sectors to help create equally spaced symbols.**

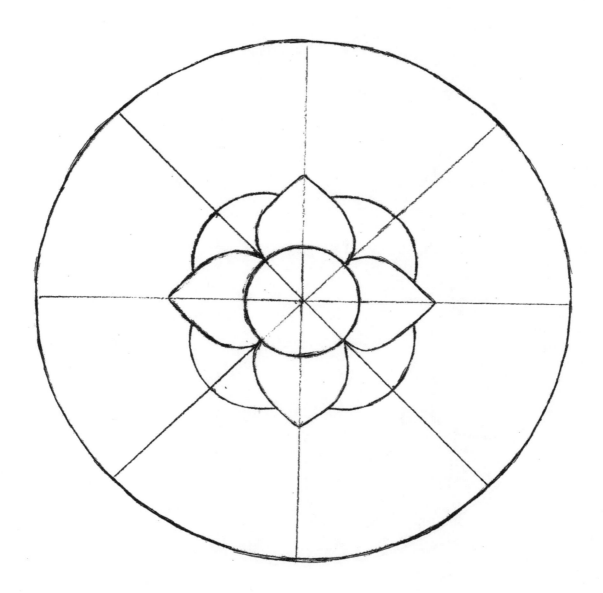

6. **Continue adding forms until you run out of space in your circle. If you elect to make your Mandala larger, simply extend the circle and carry-on. Accentuate the edges of each shape in your drawing with ink if you worked in pencil. At this point, you can now either leave the mandala as-is or continue drawing within the forms for a more complex look. Once you are satisfied with the project, erase any pencil lines that may still be showing.**

7. **Your mandala is finished and you may now proceed to color it. Claim it! Make it yours!**

Note:

As an alternative to starting with one circle as shown in step 3, you could start your mandala with a series of circles nestled within a larger circle. Then, you would add shapes within each ring.

DRAWING FROM YOUR SPIRITUAL STOREHOUSE

You are the creator, the operator, the substance, the examiner, and the user of your experimentations. Successively, devoting your attention to self-change and development will reach out to every condition and circumstance of your life.

Symbolism is priceless and deserving of your best efforts to decode its significance for symbolism has always been an effort to illustrate principles and ideas. Symbols, which when understood, feed your invisible nature. They are subtle reminders of spiritual senses of cognition by means of which the Real Self in you may be comprehended.

Yantras and Mandalas are tools that can be utilized in your meditation practices to help bring you into a higher or heightened state of awareness, an inner experience that is possible if the basic motive is to discover truth; that is to say, when you have died to caring about the outer scene and are willing to take life as it is and work from within toward your goals.

---

[1] The Vitruvian Man was drawn by Leonardo Da Vinci around 1490. The drawing is accompanied by notes based on the work of the architect Vitruvius, who correlated the ideal human proportions with geometry in his *Book III* of his treatise *De architectura*. Vitruvius described the human figure as being the principal source of proportion among the classical orders of architecture. In his drawing, Da Vinci depicts a man in two superimposed positions with his arms and legs apart and inscribed in a circle and square. The drawing and text are sometimes called the Canon of Proportions or Proportions of Man.

[2] Mantra is a Sanskrit word made up of two syllables: "man" (mind) and "tra" (liberate). Hence, in its most literal translation the word "Mantra" means, "to liberate one's mind." It does this by using a sacred message or text, charm, defined intent, counsel. Mantra could be a catchword, or a sound, such as a vowel sound repeated to aid concentration, and meditation. Mantras are also used to describe thoughts, utterances, songs, or other sequences of words or sounds producing spiritual efficacy effecting a person's will or emotional state of being.

[3] Monogram—a motif of two or more letters interwoven or otherwise combined in a decorative design, used as an emblem or to identify a personal possession.

4   Spectrograph—an apparatus for photographing or otherwise recording bands of colors (spectrum), as seen in a rainbow, produced by the separation of the components of light by their different degrees of refraction according to wavelength.

5   Initiate is a person who seeks to obtain unity with or absorption into the absolute, who through study and application can spiritually apprehend truths that are beyond the intellect.

6   Wheel of the Year is an annual cycle of seasonal festivals that consists of either four or eight celebrations: either the solstices and equinoxes, known as the "quarter days", or the four midpoints between, known as the "cross quarter days". (*en.wikipedia.org*)

This yantra is used in this book to represent our power to create our lives (as above so below), to resonate positive energies, dispense of negative ones, and to help raise our consciousness.

8

SPIRITUAL AWAKENING

MEDITATION BY SELF-ANALYSIS

Practical Application

How do you free yourself of those circumstances and conditions of earth which govern and limit you and over which you seem to have no control? The answer is simple: you shape your own life; therefore, nothing can happen to you except through your consciousness. If you are not consciously aware of something, it cannot happen to you. There may be allurements right outside your door, but if you are not aware of them, they do not touch you. There may be chances for success surging toward you, but if you do not become aware of them, they can generate nothing for you. All that touches your life must touch it through the awareness of your consciousness.

The mental process by which you make sense of yourself is by knowing the inner workings of your own mind—your internal landscape. Your spiritual Presence is standing at the door of your consciousness seeking entrance. Your mind is the door through which that Presence enters. The moment you open that door, you are flooded in its grace, in its wisdom, which comes in the form of reward, recognition, and fruitage. Thence, life has purpose and meaning because it can now express itself through you.

DISCOVERING YOUR INNER POTENTIAL

"There is no need to run outside for better seeing, nor to peer from a window. Rather abide at the center of your being; for the more you leave it, the less you learn."

Lao-Tze

You must not be afraid of the dark! As you close your eyes and turn within, you find yourself in a blackness, a darkness, but the very place where that darkness is, is your means of access to your Inner-Self, your spiritual consciousness, infinity, the endlessness and continuity of life. You must now inquire: How do you go about securing this spiritual consciousness and thereby quiet material sense? Simple, by spiritual awakening.

"Spiritual awakening is a shift in consciousness, an apperception of reality which had been previously unrealized" (*spiritualawakening.org*). You must become conscious of your own thoughts to perceive and understand. Self-analysis, in particular, our motives and character earnestly sought (by careful and deliberate effort) will reap rewards hundredfold.

You must focus your mind inwardly. What do you see? How do you feel? What are your values and beliefs? What are your behaviors and tendencies? What differentiates you from others? These are questions that elicit information to bring to the surface your level of consciousness, at that moment in time. This gives you a platform to begin working on furthering your spiritual awakening.

The typical response for all of us who are traveling our life paths in the belief that external signposts are our reality is to focus on crises, which immobilizes us; we are unable to function effectively. But, there is a valuable lesson in trials and tribulations: the experiences were a necessary step in our inner development. But, possessed by our trials and tribulations, we go on our odyssey of awakening truly convinced that the occurrences in our lives are making us unhappy. We have not yet learned that we are in a state of flux by the way our mind is processing the occurrences; hence, failing to see the benefit in the evolving set of circumstances that is our life at that moment.

As we centered inwardly and become more awakened, we use our mental faculties to build our world through peerless thinking. In examining our past events, we almost always see the benefit of our life experiences. Retrospection provides new eyes to see favorable circumstances in what was happening at an earlier stage of our life.

OUTER WORLD CONFORMING TO INNER AWARENESS

The need for retrospection minimizes as inner awareness increases. As you near this period, you become aware of favorable circumstances instantly. You stop focusing on peerless thinking of what is lacking and end catastrophizing about the future; that is, you stop irrationally thinking that something is far worse than it actually is. Instead, you shift your consciousness to realize opportunities without having to go through years of agony before seeing how compulsory events are. Simultaneously, you still experience the self-made crises, but you are able to accept yourself and trust with underlying knowingness and belief in the value of the experiences.

It involves being in present-time-consciousness to experience everything life is bringing. There is no need to spend long periods of time agonizing (replaying past events in one's mind) before becoming aware of the gift intrinsic to conflicts. Seizing the higher meaning in daily occurrences places you on the path toward true synchronicity, coexisting in harmony, in peace.

LIVING IN HARMONY

Choosing your purest thoughts offers the possibility of co-existing in context with the notion that you are mind and that your thoughts reside within and without. You can confirm this when you have the experience of knowing who is calling on the phone before you answer it. At this level of awakening, you are able to see hurdles on the horizon as simply "occurrences", which you have a choice about. You do not need to become caught up in the hurdles to have the learning experience; you simply tune-in to the Universal Mind and experience the occurrence in thought, not in form. Intuitively, you sense that to act or continue acting in a certain way is generating a forthcoming negative situation. Your intuition informs you that you are advancing toward this situation and you sense you must decide if you wish to drag yourself down this road again. When co-existing in harmony, you are able to deflect experiences in form by holding the thoughts outside the need to manifest them in form. It is literally preempting the experience rather than acquiring the knowledge through retrospection. When you allow synchronized thoughts to flow, without opposition or dismissal, their passage naturally runs its course without requiring their outer manifestation.

Having the faculty to use your mind, you can make your existence joyful and fruitful with your ability to use thought to live in harmony. The hurdles (trials and tribulations) of life are only occurrences that enable you to understand, to know your Inner-Self better. Co-existing in harmony nurtures it and it nurtures the connection to the invisible world. It enables you to start the awakening process and to become aware that by using your ability to think and analyze yourself, you fine-tune your entire life.

9

RAISING YOUR CONSCIOUSNESS

"Consciousness Is What I Am, and through Consciousness, I have Access To The Kingdom Of God, To Infinity."

Joel S. Goldsmith

"At some time in our experience, it is necessary to make a choice as to whether or not the spiritual goal is worth striving for. If we decide it is worthwhile, we will make some effort toward that consecration. We have to make the decision to practice principles of spiritual living and to remember them consciously. Then, as time goes on, this practice provides the preparation for the entrance of God into our consciousness" (*Consciousness Is What I Am*, 2).

Spiritual practice must render you calm, unruffled, poised, balanced. Beauty should be expressed in mind, emotion, and action, in thought, word and deed. This attitude toward life, naturally, entails discipline, patience and perseverance. But when directed to the task, with love and attentiveness, the endeavor is gratifying. In fact, rules and restrictions (not chaos), imposed to us by life itself, are what give attractiveness to the game of life.

In large measure, you are the creator of your own destiny. Make your thoughts cool, collected, agreeable. Be peaceful in speech, in response to animosity, to petty or unnecessary objections, to faults. One can be led astray by doubt and egotistical arguments. Praise instead. We are all bestowed with different attributes and mental faculties; so each one of us judge according to our own angle, talk and argue in the light of our own nature.

Yet, we have to stick to our rightful path, our own insights, our own determination, without getting affected by others' estimation of us. Many people do not have the capacity to judge aright, for they are full of appetites, hostility, and egotism to discern and know better, and so, they say all sorts of things. You need not to attach any value to such sayings and take them to heart, as most people do. In the end, truth always establishes itself.

Adhering to self-reliance and beneficial activities, promoting welfare and allotting others the fruits of their actions frees you from arguments and worry. Every day there should be a period in which you close your eyes, turn within, and invite God to come into your consciousness. Inasmuch as you cannot encounter a problem on the level of the problem, you must rise above the level of appearance to bring out the harmony of being. That which is open to easy view from the five senses is not the reality of things; therefore, you cannot opine from that level. Ignoring appearances, you turn from the image before the senses and begin there to become aware of Reality – of that which eternally is.

Enter the activities of the world with a new sense of reality, with a penetrating spiritual vision, which sees through the effect to its cause and knows this cause to be good. The Divine awareness within you will lead you upward and onward. Prepare yourself for the ascent. Fill your mind with spiritual realization and systematically master the art of meditation. Following is a game plan.

MODUS OPERANDI

1. Practice Meditation. The state of being awake and aware of your surroundings, your own existence, sensations, thoughts, feelings, etc. increases through meditation even if it is only for 15 minutes a day. Regularity with meditation is important; apart from that, you will find your consciousness lowering again.

2. Keep an open mind to help you learn and grow, to strengthen your belief in yourself. Be honest. There is honesty attached to being open-minded, and that is, admitting that you are not all knowing.

3. Manage your own emotional world, your emotional triggers. Let your mind be the governor, the boss of your emotions. Emotions are reactionary, they do not think. The mind strategizes and the emotions are then released by the mind to pursue its bidding.

4. Be aware of your strengths and weaknesses, virtues and vices, instabilities, caducities, and infirmities for these are your constitution as a human being.

5. Remain centered. It is only from cultivating an inner calm and centeredness that you are able to go beyond and above any outer human condition. Create a strong boundary (perimeter) to protect and keep you centered in emergency situations when you feel intense negative emotions coming from others. Pull all your energy back into yourself and behind that boundary and observe the situation from there. Do not venture across your

own boundary. As soon as you go outside of yourself, you open the door and the negative emotions from others gain entrance.

6. Accept your intuition. Follow your gut feeling. Your Higher Self desires to guide you and support you in problem solving.

7. Exercise self-discipline to control your feelings, overcome your weaknesses, and pursue what you think is right despite temptations to disregard it.

8. If your time is limited and cannot meditate daily, repeat a mantra of your choice while you go about your daily activities. It can be anything that encourages you. For example, "My good is at hand"; "I keep the doorway of my mind open to receive my goodness"; "To attract success, health, and happiness, I will eliminate fear of the future, worry over the past and anxiety for the present"; or anything you like to say that fits your specific needs.

9. Choose your activities. Your state of mind is shaped by the activities you choose each day. Choose activities that boost your spirit and stimulate right thinking and not drain your energy and weaken you. It includes choosing your working environment. Is it upbeat or low in consciousness? If low, your own mind will begin to mirror that. Get an occupation that enables you to express your full potential serving others selflessly.

10. Stay healthy. Exercise. Sun bathe (20 minutes or so daily). Feel the sun energizing you. Eat fresh vegetables, fruits, nuts, protein, good fats, vitamins, and minerals. Make daily salads your entry meal with seven to ten or more different ingredients. Make it palatable. This will give you stamina and zeal.

Purify your blood as often as possible. Your blood delivers the necessary oxygen and nutrients to the cells and transports metabolic waste products away from those same cells. The liver and kidneys make the body free of toxins all the time, but with years of use, they themselves get toxic and need cleansing. Cleansing will arouse the regenerative processes of your body.

Avoid constipation and poor digestion brought on by impure or improper combinations of foods for they will weaken the active and defensive qualities in the blood.

Practice good personal hygiene. Just think how good it feels after you take a refreshing shower and brush your teeth.

Have good posture. Maintain your spine erect, shoulders down and back, and head level to the ground. Slumping over weakens the back and keeps your energy from flowing evenly from the base of your spine to your brain. Opening the shoulders supports the movement of energy, responsibilities, and activities that need to be handled on the psychological, mental and emotional levels. The head in good posture focuses thinking, communication, and creativity. It is the major sensory activity center for your body.

11. Choose your friends. Spend time with people you admire and respect, uplift you, and make you feel happy. Sometimes though, you have to spend time with people who bring down your consciousness, such as relatives or coworkers. When this happens, minimize the time spent with them without upsetting them. While in their presence, surround yourself with white light to protect you from their negative energy.

12. Read uplifting books. Listen to or play uplifting music. Uplifting books infuses your brain with uplifting messages and positive, life-affirming concepts putting you in an optimal mindset for your day and raises your vibration. Listening to uplifting music can boost mental alertness and emotional responsiveness. A wise man once said, music is a matter of consciousness, not taste. That is to say, people like different kinds of music based on their level of consciousness. This means that if you just listen to what you feel like, you will pick music fitting to your mood, which will only hold you in the same place. If you choose something lighter and happier, you will start to feel like that. Classical or spiritual music are good choices.

13. Dress consciously. Your physical appearance influences your attitude and state of awareness. We think and function differently when we know we look nice, presentable.

14. Fast from fear to establish faith. Practice a complete abandonment to faith. This you must do for yourself. No one else can do it for you. Permit yourself to be moved upon by Divine Intelligence. Lay aside every sense of burden or false responsibility. Loose all fear and uncertainty from your thoughts and enter into your reign of good knowing that this reign is accessible to all.

15. Fast from confusion to enter into tranquility. See through all apparent contradictions to the one perfect Being in every individual.

16. Do not fear death. The moment of death is possibly the topmost point of our existence on earth, the conclusion of our life's work, and a transition from this plane of existence to another. Countless individuals, who have died and brought back by medical intervention, have corroborated to this other existence, which they described as being "more beautiful". We have also gotten strong messages about the reality of dimensions beyond the physical plane from the great spiritual masters, who have experienced them through expanded consciousness. Death is neither good nor bad. You have no alternatives in the matter. It is a finalization, which is inescapable. From the instant we are born, we are heading toward death. Some reach death sooner than others. But most people stroll along as if death is but a faraway adversity. Death is but a passing from one life to the next, a transitional movement. Your body is the car carrying your soul toward its transition and you may reach transition any moment while driving it. Make peace with it! If you remember that time is being used up every moment, you will not be enticed to waste it in empty talk

or vainglorious pursuits, cruel mischief or vulgar amusement. Travel in your vehicle cautiously, avoiding potential danger, mishap, or harm. Move calmly and with due regard for the needs of others. Know your vehicle's limitations and of the road you are travelling. Then you will not meet with any undesirable event, often physically injurious. Your travel will be a satisfying experience for you and the rest of the people on your path.

PRACTICAL APPLICATION

Testing your ideas, methods, or activities to see what effect they have in you is a way to evaluate how far you have gone into self-discovery and how far you have developed, the grandest fruit of moral victory becoming growingly real in your consciousness. See how amid the disorders of the external world you have created inner calm. See the spiritual having full play. It would be like the condense exhalation of your personality.

EPILOGUE

Whether by observation, methodical experimentation, or self-analysis, you will know you have found the best way to meditate by a growing feeling of satisfaction; by an ever-increasing peace, wisdom, and assurance from within; by a continuously progressing intuitive perception, and by an inner happiness of silence.

BIBLIOGRAPHY

Craven, Edna E., DC, CTN, BCI, ME. *Universal Mind Revealed*. Las Vegas: TopLink Publishing, 2018.

en.wikipedia.org

Gaskell, G. A. *Dictionary Of All Scriptures And Myths*. New York: Lucis Publishing Co., 1930.

Goldsmith, Joel S. *Consciousness Is What I Am*. New York, Hagerstown, San Francisco, London: Harper & Row, Publishers, 1976.

Hall, Manly P. *The Secret Teachings Of All Ages*. Los Angeles: The Philosophical Research Society, Inc. 2000.

Holmes, Ernest. *This Thing Called YOU*. New York: Dodd, Mead & Company, 1948.

Holy Bible King James Version. Nashville: Holman Bible Publishers. 1982.

Incensewarehouse.com

National Candle Association. *Fire Safety & Candles*. Washington, DC

Webster, LLD, Noah. *New Twentieth Century Dictionary* (unabridged). New York: The Publishers Guild, 1946.

CPSIA information can be obtained
at www.ICGtesting.com
Printed in the USA
BVHW020049170520
579801BV00003B/23

* 9 7 8 1 9 4 9 1 6 9 9 8 0 *